Cave Paintings to Picasso

The Inside Scoop on 50 Art Masterpieces

By Henry Sayre

chronicle books · san francisco

CONTENTS

When I was about ten years old, my family began

receiving Metropolitan Seminars in Art once a month in the mail. The series was a Book-of-the-Month Club selection, and where I grew up, it was as close as my siblings and I could get to the world of art. It was written for adults and the text was of little interest to us, but we loved the pictures. In a pocket at the front of every book was a portfolio of twelve full-color prints, and they were wonderful. We would spread them out on the floor and look at them. We would point out details to one another, wonder out loud why and how these pieces of art were painted, and sometimes even make up stories about them. Occasionally we would trace them and create our own versions of the master works with pencil and crayon. And we would ask our parents about them: Who painted the cave paintings? Who is Mona Lisa? Who is Nike and where is Samothrace? Why did Gauguin go to the South Seas? On and on—a thousand questions. Our parents did their best to

Mahana no atua:
The Art Institute of Chicago, Chicago, Illinois, U.S.A.
© The Art Institute of Chicago.

Nike of Samothrace:
Musée du Louvre, Paris, France.
© Réunion des Musées Nationaux/
Art Resource, New York.

answer, but as often as not they couldn't, and the pictures remained at least partly mysterious. Still, we learned to love art by looking at those pictures, and as we grew older we learned the stories behind them.

This book is inspired by the love, as children, that my brothers and sister and I felt for those pictures. It is, first of all, a picture book. But it is also a book of stories—stories about art that parents can read to their curious children or older kids can read for themselves, and perhaps even come away with a sense of the history of art as a whole. This book is, I hope, above all, a book of discovery, a guide to the magical wonders of the world of art.

Mona Lisa: Musée du Louvre, Paris, France.
© Erich Lessing/Art Resource, New York.

25,000 B.C.

20,000 B.C.

15,000 B.C.

10,000 B.C.

5000 B.C.

0

A.D. 5000

The *Woman from Brassempouy* is the earliest known representation of a human face. It is a tiny head just over an inch, or three centimeters, high, carved from the ivory tusk of a wooly mammoth. The period it dates from, 35,000 B.C. to 10,000 B.C., is known as the Old Stone Age because of the large number of stone tools, weapons, and figurines like this one discovered where prehistoric people used to live.

The *Woman from Brassempouy,* or the Woman in a Hood, as it is sometimes called, was discovered near Brassempouy, France, in 1984, along with a number of other small ivory figurines. Though her eyes are barely represented, the woman seems to stare out at us from beneath her strongly defined brow. Her nose is well defined, and her neck extremely long. Most interesting is her hair, which appears to be braided. It's a decorative effect has led some people to see it not as hair, but as a hood.

Almost all the surviving images of humans from prehistoric times are of women. No one knows why they were made. Many of them appear to be pregnant. (Because the body of the *Woman from Brassempouy* is missing there is no way to know whether she was represented as pregnant, but it is assumed she was.) This suggests that the figurines, which have been found all across Europe, from France to Russia, had a connection with childbearing. They may have been part of a prehistoric religion that celebrated the cycles of nature or the miracle of birth.

Woman from Brassempouy

Ivory

Height: 1¼ inches / 3 centimeters

c. 22,000 B.C.

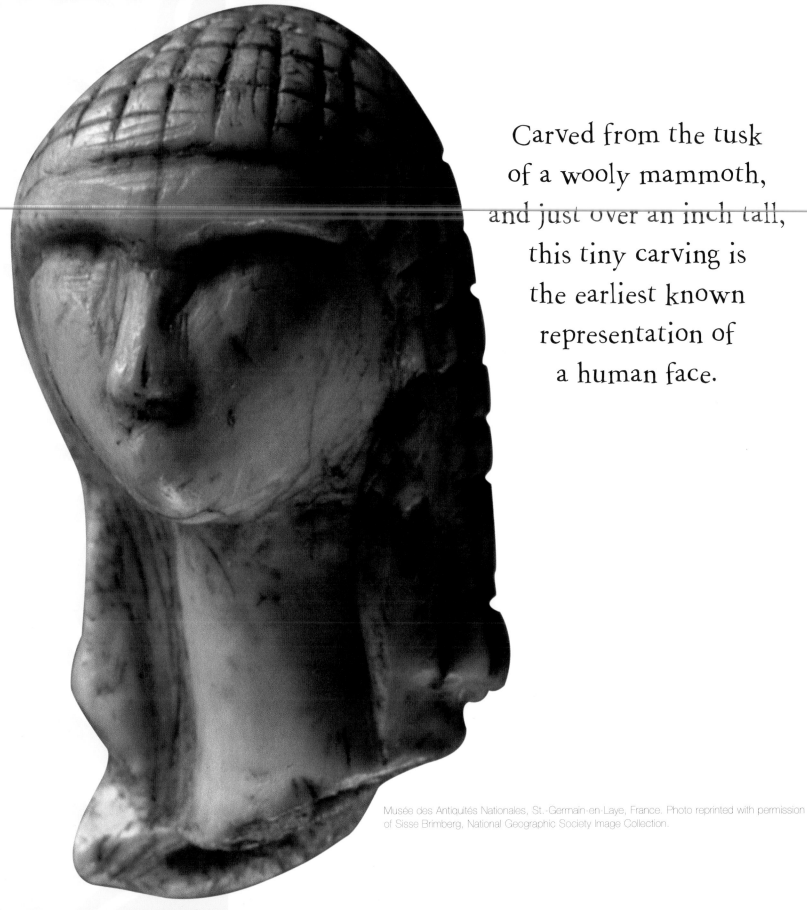

Carved from the tusk
of a wooly mammoth,
and just over an inch tall,
this tiny carving is
the earliest known
representation of
a human face.

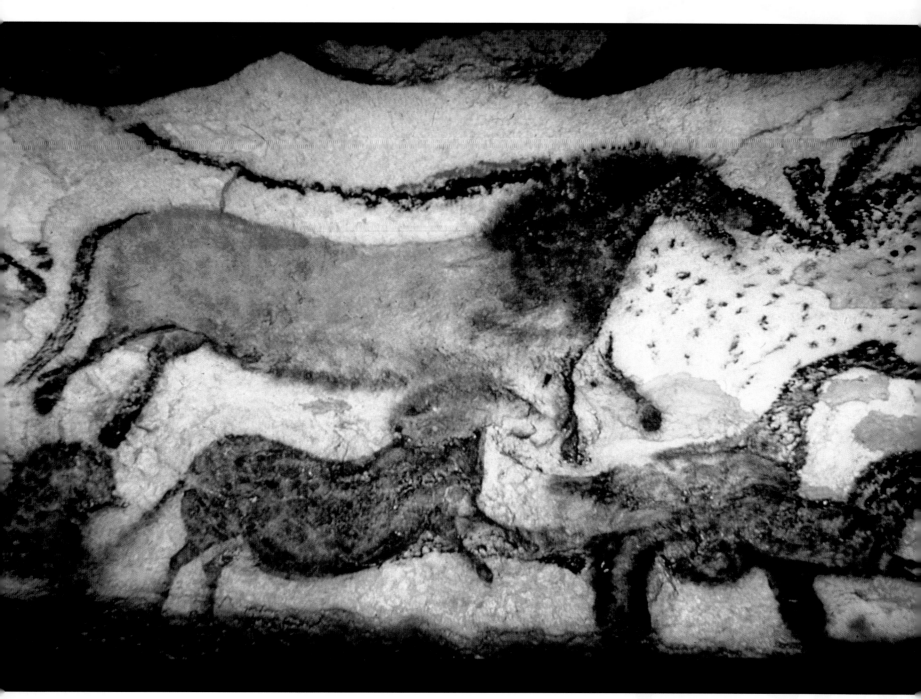

Lascaux, Dordogne, France. © Art Resource, New York.

Hall of Bulls
Lascaux, France
Cave painting
Bulls approximately life-size
c. 15,000–13,000 B.C.

One late summer day in 1938 four boys were playing with their dog outside a little town in central France. As they strolled along, their dog suddenly disappeared before their eyes. It had fallen down a hole where a tree had been uprooted in a great storm just a few years earlier. Local farmers had covered the hole with brush and branches to prevent their cattle from falling in, but the dog had not been so lucky. One of the boys lowered himself into the hole after it. The hole was not very deep, but he found himself in a long cave.

Every child in that part of France grows up knowing that caves dot the region, and that many of these caves are decorated with drawings and paintings made by people thousands of years ago. The boys thought that they might have discovered just such a cave, and so they returned the next day with a rope and a lamp and made their way deep into the cavern. Soon they came upon a large oval chamber. Its walls were covered with paintings of animals—reindeer, horses, and giant bulls.

Lascaux Cave was closed to the public in 1963 because carbon monoxide from visitors' breath was damaging the paintings. But visitors can tour an exact replica nearby.

The paintings were made with chunks of red and yellow ocher, a kind of clay, and mixed with animal fat. Scientists believe they were made between 15,000 and 17,000 years ago. The artists who made them could not read. In fact, they had no written language. But they recorded their feelings through these drawings. They may have believed that by drawing these animals they would be successful in hunting them. Or perhaps they just valued and loved the animals and drew them to honor their beauty. Whatever the case, we know from these drawings that even the most ancient peoples believed in the power of art.

Scientists believe that a huge volcanic eruption on the island of Thera, in Greece, destroyed Minoan civilization in about 1450 B.C.

On the Greek island of Crete, the great city of Knossos rose to prominence around 2000 B.C. Its inhabitants were known as Minoans, after their legendary first ruler, King Minos. The central palace of the city was enormous, and its rooms and halls were beautifully decorated with wall paintings called *frescoes.* Though we know almost nothing about the artists, they apparently believed that art should be enjoyed as part of daily life.

One of the best preserved of these Minoan frescoes is known as the *Toreador Fresco.* Three almost-nude figures appear to be toying with a charging bull. (Traditionally, as in Egyptian art, women were depicted with light skin, men with darker skin.) The woman on the left holds the bull by the horns, the man vaults over its back, and the woman on the right appears to have either just finished a vault or positioned herself to catch the man. Why would these athletes put themselves in such danger?

Bulls held a special place in Minoan culture. Their horns decorated Minoan palaces and served as drinking cups. The *Toreador Fresco* probably represents an important cultural ritual, possibly connected to the mythical Minotaur, who legend says was half man, half bull. Created by a union between Zeus, king of the Greek gods, and a mortal woman, the Minotaur was a terrible beast who instilled great fear among the Greeks until he was finally killed by a brave prince. The athletes in the *Toreador Fresco* could be symbolically reenacting the prince's victory as they perform dangerous stunts with a real bull.

Toreador Fresco

Fresco

Height: c. 32 inches including border/80 centimeters

c. 1500 B.C.

FRESCO

Fresco is a technique used for painting on walls. Wet plaster is applied to a section of a wall that is small enough to stay wet while the artist works on it. Then the artist mixes pigment (dry color) with limewater and applies the paint to the wet wall. The wet plaster soaks up the wet pigment, so the painting becomes part of the wall.

25,000 B.C.

20,000 B.C.

15,000 B.C.

10,000 B.C.

5000 B.C.

*

0

A.D. 5000

This wall painting found in the tomb of Nebamun, a member of the Egyptian nobility who died in about 1360 B.C., shows the prince standing on a small boat cruising through the marshes of the Nile River. Nebamun is identified in the hieroglyphs on the wall behind him.

Hieroglyphs, a kind of picture-writing, are one of the earliest forms of writing. If today it is hard to imagine a world without the Internet, try to imagine a world without writing. The Egyptians are among the earliest people in history that we know a lot about

because they wrote things down.

In this wall painting, Nebamun's daughter sits at his feet and his wife, stands behind him. In one hand he holds a number of birds by their feet, and in the other he draws back a throwing-stick, which he is

about to hurl at the birds rising from the reeds. His cat jumps up to bite a bird by its wing, while it grasps two others in its claws, imitating its master.

Though a beautiful scene, it is not a real one. Nebamun is enjoying the kind of perfect afternoon that Egyptians believed was attainable only in

the afterlife. Many Egyptian tombs are painted with similar scenes because Egyptians believed that after death they would be reborn into a perfect world.

British Museum, London, England. © Werner Forman/Art Resource, New York.

Nebamun Hunting Birds

Fragment of a fresco
Height: 31⁷/₈ inches/81 centimeters
c. 1400 B.C.

Queen Nefertiti has often been called the most beautiful woman in history. She was the wife of the Egyptian pharaoh Akhenaten, who ruled Egypt from 1352 to 1336 B.C. Akhenaten was fiercely independent and moved the capital of Egypt from Thebes north to Amarna. This is where, thousands of years later, the famous sculpture of Queen Nefertiti shown here was discovered.

The sculpture is a carved piece of limestone covered with plaster and then painted. The queen's swanlike neck extends forward in a graceful arc that seems to underscore her dignity.

Egyptian queens are usually shown standing dutifully beside their husbands, or admiring them as they perform great deeds (as Nebamun's wife watches him hunt). But Nefertiti is often shown by herself, and many sculptures of her, such as this one, celebrate her beauty.

Like all Egyptian women of wealth, Nefertiti probably bathed several times a day. Servants applied makeup to her face—outlining her eyes with black to make them appear larger and coloring her skin with an ochre rouge (probably the same color of the sculpture). Finally, she was dressed in a linen gown, adorned in jewelry, and crowned with an elaborate headdress.

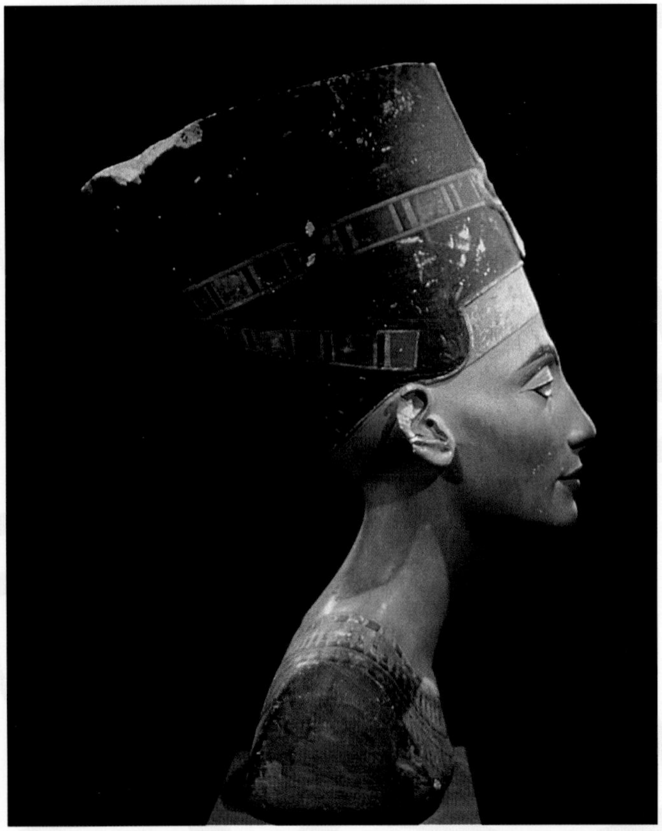

Nefertiti

Limestone, plaster, and paint
Height: 20 inches/51 centimeters
c. 1348–1336 B.C.

Soap was unknown to the Egyptians, so they washed with large salt crystals.

25,000 B.C.

20,000 B.C.

15,000 B.C.

10,000 B.C.

5000 B.C.

0

A.D. 5000

Egyptians mummified their dead because they believed that they would live again after death, and that they would need their bodies.

The tomb of King Tutankhamen—commonly referred to as King Tut—is the only royal tomb in Egypt to have escaped destruction by looters over the centuries. Tut, the son of Akhenaten, assumed the throne at age seven or eight and ruled Egypt as a child-king for eleven years from 1336 to 1327 B.C. Over time, his reign was largely forgotten, and his burial site was believed to be a small tomb containing only a few artifacts.

An English archaeologist named Howard Carter believed otherwise, and financed by the English Lord Carnarvon, he discovered King Tut's tomb in 1922. Beneath the tomb of another pharaoh, Carter found a set of steps leading to a sealed door. Drilling a hole through the door, he inserted a candle and peered inside. "At first I could see nothing," he wrote, "but presently [there appeared] strange animals, statues, and gold—everywhere the glint of gold." Crammed inside were animal-form beds of gold, chariots, shrines, chests filled with precious artifacts, and a magnificent gold and silver throne. And this was just the antechamber!

The larger tomb behind it was almost entirely filled with a giant gilded shrine. Inside it Carter discovered another shrine, and another, and another—a total of four nested shrines. In the innermost was the quartzite sarcophagus of King Tut. Its lid weighed 1.25 tons, and inside it were three golden coffins. The last one, which contained the mummy of King Tut, is made of solid gold and weighs 243 pounds, or 110.5 kilograms; the gold itself is worth approximately $1.5 million.

Pictured here is one of four miniature gold replicas of the middle coffin. Each of the four containers held Tut's preserved and embalmed internal organs, and they were encased in a separate solid-gold shrine. Lord Carnarvon never lived to enjoy the fruits of his discovery. Two weeks after entering Tut's tomb, he was bitten by a mosquito on the cheek and died from an infection soon after—the victim, the public believed, of the mummy's curse!

Burial Container for the Organs of Tutankhamen

Gold

Height: 15⅜ inches/39 centimeters

c. 1335–1327 B.C.

25,000 B.C.

20,000 B.C.

15,000 B.C.

10,000 B.C.

5000 B.C.

0

A.D. 5000

25,000 B.C.

20,000 B.C.

15,000 B.C.

10,000 B.C.

5000 B.C.

0

A.D. 5000

One of the oldest groups of people in Mexico are called the Olmecs. The Olmecs were masterful farmers. In the river valleys that flooded and refertilized the land every summer, they grew corn twice a year and many other crops.

From 1500 to 400 B.C., the Olmecs created a ceremonial center at La Venta in the heart of the river valley where they worked. La Venta's design centered around a pyramid that looked like the volcanoes that rise above the plains of Mexico. The pyramid was built on top of a giant gravel platform that was raised above the surrounding river basin. Within the platform was a huge ceremonial courtyard decorated with four giant stone heads, each seven feet, or two meters, high and weighing several tons or hundreds of kilograms. Each of these basalt stone heads wears a tight-fitting headgear, somewhat like a football helmet. Carvings on the heads indicate that they are portraits of Olmec rulers. Their giant size was probably meant to indicate the rulers' might and authority.

Colossal Olmec Head

Basalt

Height: c. 7 feet/2.1 meters

c. 800–400 B.C.

The Olmecs were the first people to discover that latex collected from rubber trees bounced. They also created the first ball game!

More than a dozen such heads have been discovered near La Venta, some of them twelve feet, or three and a half meters, high. It is a mystery how the Olmecs moved them to La Venta. The closest source for basalt stone is sixty miles south, across a vast swampland, in the Tuxtlas Mountains, where in 1960 an Olmec quarry site was discovered. This site makes clear that the monuments were probably carved into their basic round shape at the quarry site, and then rolled for sixty miles, nearly one hundred kilometers, to places like La Venta for finishing. But how did the Olmecs get them across the swamp? Today, we can only guess.

Exekias's vase is an amphora—a type of vase used to carry wine. The ancient Greeks drank wine at every meal, although it was almost always mixed with water.

Myth and legend played an important role in Greek culture, and perhaps the most important legend for the Greeks was the story of the Trojan War, which took place around 1250 B.C. In the famous story of the Trojan horse, the Greeks snuck into Troy by hiding inside a giant wooden horse that the Trojans mistook for a gift. For hundreds of years, stories associated with the Trojan War were a favorite subject for Greek painters and potters.

Over time, the Greeks perfected the use of the potter's wheel—an invention of the Egyptians, who first developed it around 4000 B.C.—which is a round, spinning platform on which clay can be easily shaped into uniform vessels. The Greeks were very skilled painters, too. They took great pride in their work, as illustrated by the fact that the vase shown here is signed on the bottom "Exekias painted me and made me."

The scene on Exekias's vase shows two Greek warriors, Achilles and Ajax, taking a break from a battle during the Trojan War to play a board game, possibly checkers. In ancient times, board games were wildly popular throughout the Mediterranean. The Egyptians were especially fond of them, and four different ivory-and-wood playing boards and many game pieces were found in King Tut's tomb. But painting nearly seven hundred years after the Trojan War, the Greek artist who created this vase shows a famous moment when the two warriors were so intent on their game that they failed to hear the goddess Athena call them to the fight. They are behaving irresponsibly, even as their friends enter into battle. Exekias tells us that even heroes are human and have weaknesses.

POTTERY DESIGN

The designs on Greek pottery were not made with paint. Potters used a special mixture of clay and water, called *slip,* to decorate the vase. In the process of firing the vase in a very hot kiln, the slip becomes black and glasslike, and the rest of the vase turns red.

Achilles and Ajax Playing a Board Game
EXEKIAS
Terracotta vase
Height: 24 inches/61 centimeters
c. 540–530 B.C.

25,000 B.C.

20,000 B.C.

15,000 B.C.

10,000 B.C.

5000 B.C.

0

A.D. 5000

23

25,000 B.C.

20,000 B.C.

15,000 B.C.

10,000 B.C.

5000 B.C.

0

A.D. 5000

The *She-Wolf* is one of the most famous animals in the history of art. For centuries she has been the symbol of the city of Rome, though she is not the work of Roman artists; she is Etruscan.

The Etruscans were a people who arrived in Italy sometime in the seventh or sixth century B.C. The region they settled, north of Rome, was extremely rich in metal ores, and they soon became renowned throughout the Mediterranean for their bronze sculptures.

The Romans loved this particular sculpture because it seemed to relate to the legend of their city's founding. In the legend, baby twins by the name of Romulus and Remus had been left to die on the banks of the Tiber River. They were rescued by a she-wolf, such as the one shown here. (The two infants were added to the sculpture more than a thousand years later during the Renaissance.) The wolf nursed the babies, saving their lives, until they were found by a shepherd. The shepherd raised them, and when the twins grew up they decided to build a city on a hill above the spot where they had been saved. But the two boys fought, and Romulus killed his brother, perhaps over who would become king of the town. That town would one day become Rome. The date, the Romans believed, was 753 B.C.

The power of the sculpture lies in the fiercely protective glare of the she-wolf's eyes, her alert ears, the way she turns to growl at any approaching danger. She was recognized by Roman citizens as a symbol of the state itself—the powerful protector of the people.

She-Wolf

Bronze
Height: 33½ inches/85 centimeters
c. 500–480 B.C.

BRONZE CASTING

First, the artist creates the sculpture in clay. He coats the sculpture with wax and coats the wax with clay. Then he fires the whole thing, and the wax melts away, leaving a narrow gap between the sculpture and the clay coating. He pours molten bronze into this gap. When it cools, he removes the clay coating and polishes the bronze.

Where the Etruscans came from remains a mystery.
The Etruscan language was not related to any other European language.

1000 B.C.

500 B.C.

*

0

A.D. 500

A.D. 1000

A.D. 1500

A.D. 2000

The *Nike of Samothrace* was discovered on the Greek island of Samothrace in the northern Aegean Sea in 1863 by French explorers who immediately took it to France. It was permanently installed at the top of a staircase in the Louvre Museum, where it has captivated viewers ever since.

The *Nike* is a winged goddess of victory. She originally stood on the prow of a sculpted stone ship that emerged from a grotto, or cave, above a two-tiered fountain on Samothrace where the island hosted several annual ceremonies, particularly a three-day festival in midsummer when large numbers of pilgrims arrived from throughout the Aegean. The sculpture was probably a memorial to a Greek naval victory in 140 B.C., but word of its beauty soon spread far and wide.

From her perch, the *Nike* overlooked the harbor and sea below. She would have seemed to the visitor to be arriving in all her majesty, the wind blowing back her gowns, her wings balancing her against the force of the gale. Her right arm—never found, though the hand survives—would have been raised above her head in victory.

She was carved from a giant block of marble. And yet it is not cold, hard stone that we feel when we see her. Rather we feel the rush of air that surrounds her, the salt spray from the sea that causes her garments to cling to her body. She is not the only subject mastered by the unknown artist who sculpted her; he also mastered the environment that envelops her, the air in which she seems magically to live.

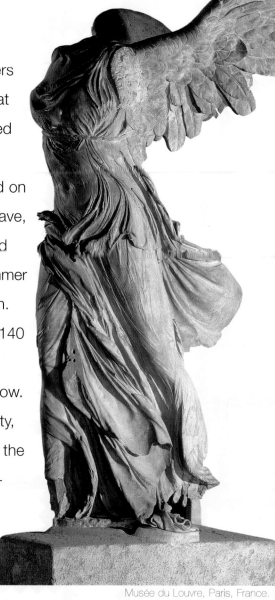

Musée du Louvre, Paris, France.
© Réunion des Musées Nationaux/Art Resource, New York.

Nike of Samothrace

Marble
Height: 8 feet/2.4 meters
c. 140 B.C.

Between A.D. 200 and 700, along the Pacific coast of Peru, a people known as the Moche lived and worked. We know very little about them—no written record survives—but they were very skilled artists and architects.

They lived together in giant flat-topped *huacas,* or pyramids, made of bricks and clay mud. The largest of these was the Huaca del Sol, the Pyramid of the Sun, which was also used as a burial site. Seventeenth century gold seekers found many bodies buried there along with gold artifacts, which they took.

The Moche were great ceramic artists. Their favorite design was a bottle with a stirrup-shaped spout. Many such bottles were buried with the dead at Huaca del Sol, but the gold-crazed Spaniards didn't care about them.

Here, a king in ceremonial headdress, petting a baby jaguar, decorates the top of a bottle. That the king has a jaguar, the fiercest of all animals known to the Moche, as a pet shows the king's power and strength. The Moche put all kinds of decorations on their bottles—the model of a house, a portrait of a loved one, warriors doing battle, children playing—and it is only from these that we know anything about Moche culture.

By A.D. 800 the Moche people had disappeared without a trace. Evidence suggests that a large earthquake may have blocked the Moche River, leaving them waterless. The climate also may have changed dramatically, destroying their food supply. They may have moved northward and joined Central American and Mexican populations, but if they did, they left the art of their unique stirrup-spouted bottles behind forever.

Moche Lord with a Feline

Painted ceramic
Height: 7½ inches/19.1 centimeters
c. 100 B.C.–A.D. 500

THE HORSES OF SAN MARCO are so large, they had to be cast in pieces. The pieces were then pounded together to make each horse.

The Horses of San Marco

Gilt-bronze

Life-size

c. A.D. 100–200

The Horses of San Marco have galloped on a wild journey through history. They were originally Greek or Roman, and were created as an example of a Roman *quadriga*—the four horses that pulled Roman chariot racers. In A.D. 324, when the Roman Emperor Constantine moved the capitol of the Roman Empire from Rome to Constantinople (present-day Istanbul, in Turkey), he carried these horses with him. He installed them in his personal box at the Hippodrome, a giant center of public entertainment devoted to chariot races and contests among gladiators. There they stood for nearly nine hundred years, proudly watching over the athletic contests of the emperors.

In 1204 troops from the city of Venice looted Constantinople in order to destroy its chief rival for sea trade in the Mediterranean. Among the wealth of gold, gemstones, and art the Venetian troops carried away were the four magnificent bronze horses. In order to fit them on the ship for their journey back to Venice, their heads were cut off. The collars they wear today were added by the Venetians to hide the cuts. In Venice they were quickly stationed atop the entrance of St. Mark's Basilica, and in this context, their meaning changed. In Constantinople they were images of physical prowess and strength. But adorning the main entrance of St. Mark's Basilica, they became the horses of the four Christian evangelists—Matthew, Mark, Luke, and John.

And then in 1797 the French Emperor Napoleon Bonaparte defeated Venice in battle and the horses again traveled to another city. This time they went to Paris, but their stay there was short-lived. When Napoleon was defeated at Waterloo in 1815, the French returned them to Venice, where now, almost two hundred years later, they can still be found.

1000 B.C.

500 B.C.

0

*

A.D. 500

A.D. 1000

A.D. 1500

A.D. 2000

1000 B.C.

500 B.C.

0

A.D. 500

A.D. 1000

A.D. 1500

A.D. 2000

The *Book of Kells* is one of the most beautiful of all illustrated books. It was made in the last half of the eighth century by Irish monks on the remote island of Iona off Scotland. It contains the four gospels of the Bible's New Testament—the books of Matthew, Mark, Luke, and John.

In Ireland in the Middle Ages, work in a monastery was carried out in silence, and bookmaking was the chief occupation. Unlike today, when printing presses can turn out thousands of books a day, in the Middle Ages books were made by hand, one at a time, with pen and brush, and took thousands of hours to finish. Because paper would not be used for several centuries, the books were written on animal skins, or vellum.

Book of Kells
Tempera illustration on vellum
13 x 9½ inches/33 x 25 centimeters
c. 750–800

The Board of Trinity College, Dublin, Ireland, MS 58 (A.1.6.), fol. 34v.
© Art Resource, New York.

The page shown here begins the story of Jesus's birth from the gospel of Matthew. There are only three words on the page: "Christ is born." The largest illustrations are three Greek letters: *X, P,* and *I,* which stand for Christ. But look closely and you will see an otter with a fish, a peacock, three angels, two cats with mice on their backs, and a red-haired boy who may represent Jesus.

The *Book of Kells* was moved to Ireland after Vikings attacked Iona in 878. In 1006 it was stolen for its gold and jewel-encrusted cover. Months later, it was found buried in a bog. Though lacking its cover, it was in relatively good condition, and this "miracle" proved to many its great worth.

Easter Island Ancestor Figures

Volcanic stone (tufa)
Average height: c. 36 feet/11 meters
c. 1000–1500 (restored 1978)

1000 B.C.

500 B.C.

0

A.D. 500

A.D. 1000

*

A.D. 1500

A.D. 2000

No one knows how or why the Polynesians came to inhabit the islands of the South Pacific. Without compasses or maps, in canoes filled with bundles of dried food, gourds of fresh water, pigs, dogs, and seeds for planting, these settlers sailed across the ocean for islands that they could not have known existed. Sometime after A.D. 500, they reached Easter Island, the most remote of all the Polynesian islands. About five hundred years later, for reasons no one knows, they began to erect giant stone figures along the hillsides of the island in lines parallel to the coast. These figures may have been memorials to dead chiefs, or guardians against hurricanes and storms.

Nearly a thousand of these stone figures, called *moai,* have been found. Carved of a volcanic stone called *tufa,* most are about thirty-six feet, or ten meters, high, though some are twice that height.

Sometime around 1500, the Easter Islanders stopped making these monuments. It seems likely that the people had used up the island's natural resources. There was a period of warfare as islanders competed for what was left, and most of the *moai* were knocked down and destroyed.

One hundred statues were carved but never erected by the Islanders. They still lie partway to their destination. No one knows why.

Easter Island, Polynesia Islands, Chile. © Erich Lessing/Art Resource, New York.

1000 B.C.

500 B.C.

0

A.D. 500

A.D. 1000

A.D. 1500

A.D. 2000

The Bayeux Tapestry

Linen and wool tapestry
Height: 20 inches/50.8 centimeters
c. 1070–80

The Bayeux Tapestry is an embroidered fabric 230 feet, or 70 meters, long and 20 inches, or 50 centimeters, high—an ancient example of a kind of storytelling that we see every day in the newspaper: the comic strip. It was sewn between 1070 and 1080, most likely by women at the School of Embroidery at Canterbury, in Kent, England. It was sewn in three large pieces that were stitched together, and for centuries it was hung around the altar of Bayeux Cathedral on feast days and special occasions.

The Bayeux Tapestry tells the story of the conquest of England in 1066 by William, Duke of Normandy. When the English King Edward died on January 5, 1066, he did not have an heir, and William, who lived across the English Channel in France, claimed the throne. He swore that King Edward had promised it to him. But Harold of Wessex claimed that on his deathbed Edward had named *him* king and so he took the throne. So William went to England to try to defeat Harold.

In the first section of *The Bayeux Tapestry* shown here, Harold sits on the throne of England. But all is not well. Overhead, a huge comet appears in the sky—in fact, Halley's Comet, which passes

the earth every seventy-five or seventy-six years (the last time in 1986). To the left, townspeople point and stare, since it is a bad omen for King Harold. In the next section, the Normans sail to England in boats with animal-head prows, showing their Viking ancestry. In the last section, a Norman rider with a sword strikes down Harold at the Battle of Hastings. The Latin words above the scene tell us that "Harold the king is killed." And so the Normans won the battle, and William became king of England.

There are 623 humans, 202 horses, 41 ships, and over 500 other creatures, ranging from birds to dragons, in THE BAYEUX TAPESTRY.

Centre Guillaume le Conquérant, Musée de la Tapisserie, Bayeux, France. © Erich Lessing/Art Resource, New York

Many Chinese landscapes show mist, fog, and clouds, which represent the life force, called the qi in Chinese.

Calligraphy—the art of handwriting—and landscape painting have traditionally been considered the two highest forms of art in Chinese culture. Calligraphy expresses the character of the artist. Landscape painting captures the truth that lies in nature. Guo Xi's painting *Early Spring* shows that both calligraphy and landscape painting are closely related. The painting is based on the Chinese character for mountain:

山

The tall peak rises in the middle, surrounded by lesser peaks on each side. Both calligraphy and painting capture what it means to be a mountain.

But Guo Xi is interested in telling us much more. Guo Xi told his son, Guo Si, that the forests, streams, and mountains all contain "messages." The mountain in *Early Spring,* rising high above the landscape below, is like the Chinese emperor, who rises above his people. The surrounding mountains are like his close advisors, and the pine trees their best ideas and good works. The common people in this painting are small and insignificant. Two figures get out of their boat at the bottom left, and another figure stands on the shoreline at the right. A small village can be seen nestled on the mountainside above the waterfalls. All are dwarfed by the giant mountain.

Guo Xi painted *Early Spring* so that viewers gaze up at the mountain, as they would properly look up to the emperor.

INK PAINTING

When working with ink, the artist uses firm strokes to make dark outlines and crisp lines. To create a look of moisture or fog, he retraces the crisp line several times with an ink wash (watered-down ink) that blurs the line.

Early Spring
GUO XI
Hanging scroll, ink and slight color on silk
Length: 5 feet/1.59 meters
1072

1000 B.C.

500 B.C.

0

A.D. 500

A.D. 1000

＊

A.D. 1500

A.D. 2000

1000 B.C.

500 B.C.

0

A.D. 500

A.D. 1000

A.D. 1500

A.D. 2000

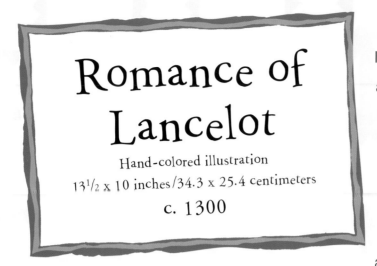

Romance of Lancelot

Hand-colored illustration
13½ x 10 inches/34.3 x 25.4 centimeters
c. 1300

In the twelfth century, across Europe, poems and stories recounting the love of knights for their ladies, called "courtly love," became extremely popular. *The Romance of Lancelot,* written by Chrétien de Troyes around 1170 for Marie, the daughter of Eleanor of Aquitane, Queen of England, was the most popular of all. It was published many times, often with illustrations like the one reproduced here. It tells of the adventures of Lancelot, a knight in the court of the legendary King Arthur, and his love for the lady Guinevere.

Scholars still wonder if Camelot was a real place.

When the story opens, Guinevere has been kidnapped. Lancelot sets off to rescue her. Along the way, he encounters many trials and challenges, from sword fights to the most fearsome challenge of them all, the trial of the "sword-bridge," which is shown here. It crosses a "wicked-looking stream…swift and raging…fierce and terrible…so dangerous and bottomless that anything falling into it would be completely lost." The bridge itself is a polished sword, its blade stuck into a tree trunk at each end. Its blade is turned upward, "sharper than a scythe," and Lancelot knows that it will cut him as he creeps across it on his hands and knees. But across the way, Lancelot can see the lady Guinevere standing in a tower. "Even his suffering is sweet to him" with Guinevere in sight. No obstacle seems too great. Every agony seems worth suffering. Thus he finally reaches the other side and rescues his love, though, in fact, his adventures have just begun.

la vie ouez; ſire fait cil qui deſcouuſſ ne v̈ veult pas ie ne ſuis mie cil veurs p̓ moy herbergier a ceſte heure; ſi m̓ a on fait entendre que ie me doy a i. chlr combatre; ſe il eſt ci qi vaincre deuant; car mlt de fiz q̓ ie men ſuis deliures; Bian ſire fait li ̃bons; ne vos haſtez ſi de la bataille; car vos nen aues; mie mlt grāt meſtier a ceſtui point ainz vos ſeiornerez; huimais aẽc voſtre pl̓ eſpoir; Et ſe len vos vendoit ſans bataille ce que vos eſtes venus; q̃re; Blauerez; plus ligerement; Et ſe le vorroie bñ le ſathez; car v̈ eſter li hons ou monde por cui ie ſeroie plus; Por moy biau ſire fait lanc̃

le p̓ vos garantir mõ; car v̈ naues pa le poou̓ ẽtre celui qui te doit combatre auoſ; ſe ie ne vos plaiſt encõduir; Et ie vos pdour de lore mais; Et vos ſerai garãir cõtre tout homes; loꝛs dun̄ z de vꝛe bataille q̓l q̓ auerez; demain; car auꝛz ̃uel poꝛes; vos auoir; qi iaiz montes; loꝛ ceſt cheual; z fu meſt bons ie vos douŋ nulloꝛz alles; Et il le vout al dit q̓ le vos amg̓ mez; zchlr qui ſoit ou monde; cil q̓ la grāt proeſſe; qui eſt en vos; lant dit li ꝛons̄ mauŋ; qui eſt mõtez; ſi en vout grāt aleure en la cire ſilo fait li ꝛois entrer en la plus celee chambre qui ſoit leans ſina reine; aẽc lui de toute gent que y ſeul eſcuier qui ſera ce que

pꝛiſonnieꝛs; Et ailz a dire ceſte parſõ;

IL deſcendu loꝛ fait qꝛleagant ne voſſcmnay; z bū peuꝛ ſil cueꝛz voſſeſt kanus; qͦt poꝛla douce dun ſeul chlr; me coullliez a ſaiꝛe plait dont ie me honniſſe; Dꝛ ce fait li ꝛois̄ ne ſ̃roie̓ ia hõnz; ainz encõgꝛourze pꝛz; z honoꝛ; car tout li mõde̓ dirant q̃tu auerioꝛes quite ce que tu auerioꝛes oquiſ par proeſſe; Et ce ſeroit grāt pꝛz z grāt hõnoꝛs; Certez fait cil ie non moŋ point; aintoul ſeroit grāt couardie; Si uiſ bien que voſ eſter kanus cuer; ou vos doutez; celui ou auoŋ me haez; qui cume d̃nez auſeil di moy haũſ; ſe la ꝛce ſe ceil lanc̃

e ſauge pꝛay voz veũez tant; car ne ſui ouquez de voul acouter ne oſ z nuy; ſe ie ne voſ ui ouquez ũ mieŋ cuidieꝛ; mar quez que ie ne fences moy ma bataille auoŋ ꝛ ie la del ſe ouq̓ pboute que ie atendiſſe aamoꝛ de alloing neuuŋ par p̓ gꝛaingue faire auꝛ p̓auereŋ mŋ ̃dhez lec engẽtemn loꝛs; li ꝛois̄ utent bien qͦl le ſaute vl̓ nuy poꝛ voꝛ paour deſtꝛe queŋz; Si bee aꝛ ſaire outremenent qͦ qͥl cuidera ꝛ ou li ſire;

ſꝛe chlr eune ſan qui v̈ eſtez bū le ſathez; ſle ia en ma iauby ne voſ ſera nuz ſoꝛe deŋ voſ mouſtꝛe; ſle ie ne vos del bbgͣrŋ

li gͤmaudin; Et ſe gard ſl m̄ uuez entrer leans; poꝛ ce que deſcourŋ nele velte mie ne courotier; A pꝛes eſt li ꝛonc̄ venuz aiſſou fil; z li dut; Bianz̄ Roy tuaz veut maŋ bel chlr; puiſ que tu veuz armel poꝛter mais tu ne veꝛz ouquez mais nul ſi apertement hardi q̄me cil eſt quil a huŋ paſſer le pont; zp̓ le grāt hardement que noꝛ y auoms̄ veu te bõuoꝛege que tu ſ̃uatez tant que tu y euꝛſz honoꝛ atone voꝛ mais; Que me loez; voꝛ fait ayeleagaŋz; que ̃ou enfãce; Ie te dꝛay fait li ꝛonc̄ que ie te loeroie; que tu tiꝛo duſſes la ꝛoine outremenent; car tu mar dit̄z enu uenir; ſle en nuil deꝛ

ſie me eſpoente; car iai aſſez zeŋ er z ſoꝛce deŋ lui acendre; z de obaŋ gꝛe luŋ; Et ſe vos lauez hbergue contre moy; tant auerage pl̓ grāt honoꝛ; enma droiture deſſendre Et enceil lui ſauge ahati na ̃gauꝛe on ſl auoit plus dauŋz z de ſecoꝛs quil naueꝛa ce; car ceſtui enla ̃coꝛt le ꝛoy artu;

Comēt fait li ꝛonc̄ ſeᷓu que ce ſoit lanc̄; par la ſoy que ie doy a qui me eſt fil; ꝛez; ie ne ſay chu il eſt neſ que tu ſayz; car ie ne lay encoꝛe veut ſ̃ arme noŋ; Mais ſe ie ſauoie deŋ voir q̃e ſuſt lanc̃ Tu ne te obaterouꝛŋ a luŋ; car tu ni poꝛrouꝛ auoir durꝛe; Ouͣquez

In the Middle Ages, Muslims made many important discoveries and inventions, including Arabic numbers, which quickly replaced Roman numerals.

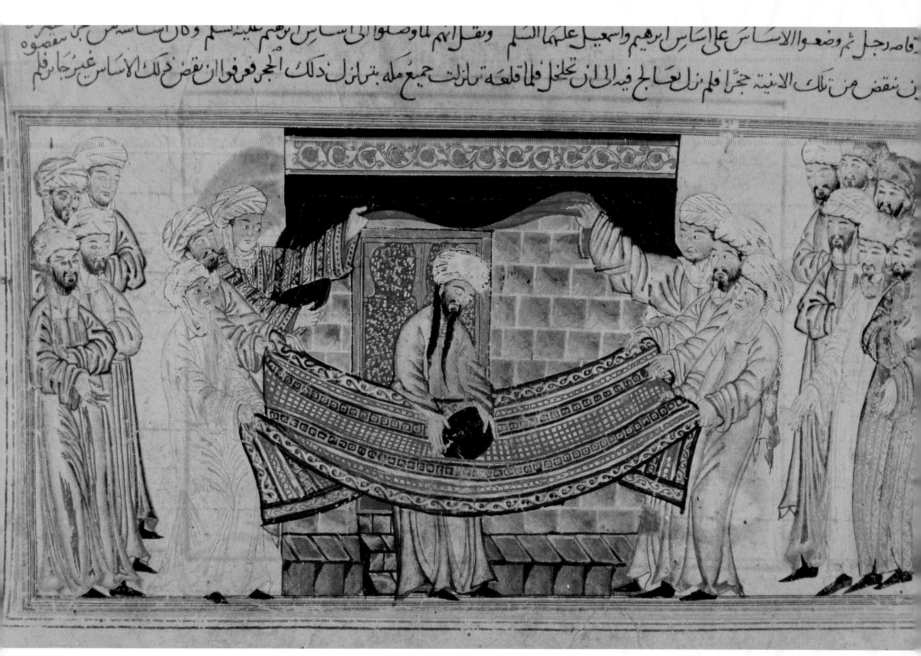

Mecca is the birthplace of Muhammad, the great prophet of Islam. At the age of forty, in 610, Muhammad heard a voice—the angel Gabriel's, as the story goes—urging him to "recite." He responded, "What shall I recite?" And for the next twenty-two years, until his death, he claimed to receive messages from God through Gabriel. These he memorized and told to scribes, who collected them to form the scriptures of Islam, the Qur'an (or Koran), which means "recitations."

Muhammad is the ideal Muslim, and all Muslims model their life on his. The illustration here recounts the story of the rebuilding of the Kaaba, a building in the center of Mecca. Muslims believe that the Kaaba (literally "cube") is the site of the first "house of God," built at God's command. The Kaaba housed the sacred Black Stone that reportedly "fell from heaven." (It is probably a meteorite.) In 630 Muhammad ordered the Kaaba rebuilt and cleansed. When workmen were ready to replace the Black Stone in the newly cleansed Kaaba, a quarrel broke out among the main Arab tribes because each wanted the privilege of laying the stone in place. Finally everyone agreed that the first passerby would have the honor. That passerby turned out to be Muhammad, who placed the stone on his cloak and then gave a corner to the head of each tribe to carry into the Kaaba. All equally shared in the honor, thanks to Muhammad's great wisdom.

Muhammad Placing the Black Stone on His Cloak

Hand-colored illustration
5 1/8 x 10 1/4 inches / 13 x 26 centimeters
1315

1000 B.C.

500 B.C.

0

A.D. 500

A.D. 1000

A.D. 1500

A.D. 2000

In the late Middle Ages, between about 1150 and 1300, Siena, Italy, was one of the most powerful cities in Europe. Its citizens believed that Siena's success was a result of the fact that it was governed well. So in 1338 they commissioned the painter Ambrogio Lorenzetti to paint two frescoes in the council chamber of Siena's city hall. On three walls was *The Allegory of Good Government: the Effects of Good Government in the City and the Country.* Across the chamber, Lorenzetti also painted *The Allegory of Bad Government: the Effects of Bad Government in the City.*

The Effects of Good Government

AMBROGIO LORENZETTI

Fresco
Length: 46 feet/14 meters
1338–39

Ten years after Lorenzetti painted this work, the Black Plague ravaged Europe. It killed 65,000 of Siena's 100,000 citizens.

The Effects of Good Government shows richly dressed merchants dancing in the street, one couple passing beneath the arching arms of another, followed by a chain of other revelers dancing hand in hand. To the left, in an arched portico, three men engage in a board game. They have leisure time. To their right is a shoe shop; behind that is a schoolroom where a teacher helps her students learn; and beside the schoolroom is a wine shop. At the very top of the painting, masons construct a new building. Outside the gate, to the right, the surrounding countryside is depicted in all its lushness. Farmers bring livestock and produce to market; workers till the fields and labor in the vineyards. Above them all, floating in the sky, is the nearly nude figure of *Securitas*—"Security"—carrying a gallows in one hand and a scroll in the other, reminding the citizens that peace depends upon justice.

In 1279 the Mongol warrior Kublai Khan, grandson of the famous Genghis Khan, invaded China. During the summers, he lived in Xanadu, a luxurious city known for its beautiful lakes and gardens. It was at this summer court that the Venetian adventurer Marco Polo met Kublai Kahn. Marco Polo's description of the magnificent lifestyle of Kublai Khan's court was for many centuries the only information about China available in Europe.

The capital of China in Wu Chen's time, Hangzhou, was the largest city in the world. Its two million inhabitants lived surrounded by 30-foot-high walls.

Bamboo

WU CHEN

Album leaf, ink on paper
16 x 21 inches/40.6 x 53.5 centimeters
1350

But many of the scholar-painters of the Chinese court were unwilling to serve under Kublai Khan because he was a foreigner. They secretly tried to keep traditional Chinese values and arts alive.

The bamboo in Wu Chen's painting was a political symbol aimed at the hated Mongol rulers. Bamboo bends, but it does not break. The artist wanted to show that China would bend under foreign rule, but it would not give in to it.

The painting's calligraphy is another attempt by Wu Chen to honor the memory of China before the coming of Kublai Kahn. He chose a style of writing developed in the eighth century. It is intentionally loose and free. Wu Chen meant it to symbolize Chinese freedom.

In 1368 the Mongols were finally overthrown when Zhu Yuanzhang drove the last Mongol emperor north into the desert and declared himself first emperor of the new Ming dynasty. China was once again ruled by the Chinese.

1000 B.C.

500 B.C.

0

A.D. 500

A.D. 1000

A.D. 1500

A.D. 2000

1000 B.C.

500 B.C.

0

A.D. 500

A.D. 1000

A.D. 1500

A.D. 2000

January, Les Très Riches Heures

LIMBOURG BROTHERS

Illustration on parchment
8³/₃₄ x 5⁵/₁₆ inches/22.2 x 13.5 centimeters

c. 1415

Musée Condé, Chantilly, France.
Photograph reprinted with permission of R. G. Ojeda, Musée Condé.

The Duke of Berry was a French nobleman who lived around 1400 and was one of richest men in the world. He loved animals, and at his castle near Paris he created his own private zoo. His two favorite dogs, little Pomeranians, went with him everywhere, and so did a pair of bears. The duke also loved books. He hired three great artists—the brothers Paul, Herman, and Jean Limbourg—to make him an illustrated "book of hours," a monthly calendar that contains the "hours" of prayer. The book is so lavish that its French title translates as "The Very Rich Book of Hours." Precious metals and stones were ground to make the paint, including two pouches of a valuable blue stone called *lapus lazuli.*

The beautiful blues are especially apparent in this illustration for January 1413. The Duke of Berry sits at a banquet table dressed in a deep blue robe and a fur cap. On the wall behind him hang tapestries showing the Trojan War, transformed into a medieval battle. It is New Year's Day, the traditional day for the giving of gifts. (Christmas wouldn't take that role until the nineteenth century.)

New arrivals are greeted by the duke's chamberlain, the man in charge of the duke's living quarters, who says, *"Approche, approche!"*—"Come in, come in!" Behind them is a self-portrait of one of the artists, which suggests that the illustration is a real scene. Perhaps the artists enjoyed the feast that day as much as the Duke's two Pomeranians, who freely roam about the table.

Camera Picta
ANDREA MANTEGNA

Fresco
Diameter of balcony: 5 feet/1.52 meters
1474

1000 B.C.

500 B.C.

0

A.D. 500

A.D. 1000

A.D. 1500

A.D. 2000

In 1465 Ludovico Gonzaga, the extremely wealthy marquis of the small northern Italian town of Mantua, asked his court painter, Andrea Mantegna, to decorate a room on the first floor of his castle with wall-to-wall frescoes. It would come to be called the *Camera Picta,* or "Room of Pictures," and would take Mantegna nearly ten years to complete.

The room itself served two purposes. At night Ludovico and his wife used it as their bedchamber. By day, it was Ludovico's business office, where he received visiting dignitaries, conducted affairs of state, and consulted with his advisers.

On the walls, Mantegna painted images of Ludovico and his family doing business. But the ceiling is very different. It is painted as if there were a round opening—called an *oculus,* or eye—revealing a bright summer sky. The opening is surrounded by a balcony, where there are four ladies of the court, what appears to be their maid, a peacock, and numerous *puti,* or winged baby angels. A potted orange tree is perched over the balcony railing on a stick. Several of the *puti* have poked their heads through the railing, and at least one seems stuck. Three others have stepped over the railing. The *puti* all represent innocence, but they also show that the innocent do not always behave wisely.

Why would Mantegna paint the ceiling with such a silly scene? The peacock gives us a clue. The beautiful bird traditionally represents vanity. When Ludovico conducted his business, the figures on the ceiling reminded him not to take himself too seriously.

Palazzo ducale, Mantua, Italy. © Scala/Art Resource, New York.

1000 B.C.

500 B.C.

0

A.D. 500

A.D. 1000

A.D. 1500

*

A.D. 2000

The peacock is the oldest of all ornamental birds, introduced into the cultures of the Middle East more than four thousand years ago. For hundreds of years, peacocks were traded to the Chinese in exchange for silk, a material spun by silkworms fed on mulberry leaves, which until about A.D. 600, only the Chinese knew how to make.

> ## Hundreds of Birds Admiring the Peacocks
> ### YIN HONG
> Hanging scroll, ink and color on silk
> 7 feet, 10¹/₂ inches x 6 feet, 5 inches
> 2.4 x 1.96 meters
> #### c. 1550–1650

So it is no accident that *Hundreds of Birds Admiring the Peacocks* is painted on silk. Silk is the material of the Chinese emperors. Soft and beautiful, it reflects light like the shiny feathers of the peacock itself. In fact, the peacock, with its tail feathers of bright blue and green, each with a design near its tip that looks like an eye, became for the Chinese a symbol of beauty and elegance. It also became a symbol of the emperor. In the painting, the birds flock around it in admiration. It is as beautiful as the flowers in the garden and the blossoms in the cherry tree, as noble and enduring as the ancient willow trees that stand by the flowing river. Symbolically, the river shows time flowing by. The peacock/emperor will give shade and cover for the hundreds of birds—symbols of the masses of people—who admire and follow it.

In this sense, life under the Chinese emperors is shown here as nearly perfect—the people, or birds, gather in a garden setting where nothing can interrupt the quiet and peaceful harmony of their contentment.

The Cleveland Museum of Art, Cleveland, Ohio, U.S.A. Purchase from the J.H. Wade Fund, 74.11. Photograph reprinted with permission of the Cleveland Museum of Art.

Sight

Wool and silk tapestry
10 feet, 2 inches x 10 feet, 10 inches
3 x 3.3 meters
c. 1550–1600

In the late Middle Ages, tapestries were the most sought-after works of art in Europe. They decorated the walls of castles and were prized not only for their beauty but for their warmth, since they insulated rooms from stone walls that were often colder than the temperature outside. Tapestries typically had backgrounds full of flowers and small animals, a style known as *millefleurs,* or "a thousand flowers." They were often made in groups of four, five, or six, so that taken together they might tell a story or create a scene, which would give the rooms they decorated a common theme.

One of the most famous of these groups is known as the Five Senses Tapestries or as the Lady and the Unicorn series. It was created for a French family whose crests featured two emblems—the lion, for its strength, and the unicorn, for its swiftness. Legend had it that the unicorn could be tamed only by a beautiful lady. In each of the first five tapestries, the lady uses one of the five senses to bring the unicorn under her power. Here, in the tapestry *Sight,* the lady holds up a mirror so that the unicorn can admire itself, suggesting that the unicorn is in love more with itself than with any other. Finally, in the sixth tapestry, the lady seems to reject the world of the senses—tears are in her eyes as she takes off the beautiful necklace that she has worn in all the other scenes and places it in a jewelbox. She has learned the lesson that the world of the senses and the enjoyment of beautiful things is less important than love itself, which is the most powerful force of all.

Musée du Moyen Age (Cluny), Paris, France. Inv.: CL 10836.
Photograph: R.G. Ojeda. © Réunion des Musées Nationaux/
Art Resource, New York.

1000 B.C.

500 B.C.

0

A.D. 500

A.D. 1000

A.D. 1500

✱

A.D. 2000

1000 B.C.

500 B.C.

0

A.D. 500

A.D. 1000

A.D. 1500

A.D. 2000

Primavera
SANDRO BOTTICELLI

Tempera on a gesso ground on poplar panel
6 feet, 8 inches x 10 feet, 3½ inches
2.03 x 3.15 meters
c. 1482

Sandro Botticelli's *Primavera* (which is Italian for "spring") was probably painted for the wedding chamber of Lorenzo de' Medici, the most powerful man in Florence, Italy, in the fifteenth century and one of the greatest patrons in the history of art. The painting is very large and the figures in it are life-size. In the center, the goddess Venus is the symbol of spring. She stands under an arch of fruit-laden trees on a carpet of flowers reminiscent of the *millefleurs* tapestries of the Middle Ages. Cupid, with a flame-tipped bow, flies above her head, readying to shoot his arrow of love. Where it will land, not even Cupid knows, since he is blindfolded—love, as they say, is blind.

The painting reads from right to left. To the right, Zephyr, the cold, blue wind of early spring, tries to capture a nymph and bring her under winter's spell. But she escapes into the bower and transforms into Flora, the spirit of spring. Venus, in the center, gestures as if inviting the Three Graces, farther left, to commence their dance. Their dance is a celebration of a new world, the world of spring, still pure and untainted by evil. Finally, on the far left, Mercury, the god of May, reaches upward with his staff and shoos the last clouds of spring away, as he turns toward the summer months to come.

To create his painting, Botticelli first outlined the trees and human figures and then painted the sky. He used an undercoat of white for the figures and an undercoat of black for the trees. He imitated the transparency of drapery by layering as many as thirty coats of thin yellow washes of clear paint over the white undercoat.

TEMPERA PAINTING

Botticelli's painting is done in *tempera*, made of water, color pigment, and a gummy substance such as egg yolk. It is applied with the point of fine sable brush to a very smooth surface, usually covered with *gesso*, made from glue and plaster of Paris.

As a youth, Botticelli was a poor student, so his father took him out of school and apprenticed him to a goldsmith, which is how he learned to paint with the precise lines that goldsmiths use to decorate their work.

When the DAVID was completed, it took forty men sixty days to move the sculpture to its place in the central square of Florence.

Michelangelo's great sculpture *David* is considered a masterpiece of Renaissance art. It represents the biblical story of David's triumph over the giant tyrant Goliath. The sculpture depicts
David in the moment before the battle. Over his shoulder, David carries his slingshot, which he
will soon use to bring down Goliath, as he regards the approaching giant with supreme confidence.

The *David* Michelangelo sculpted is a giant itself. It stands nearly thirteen and a half feet,
or four meters, high, and on its pedestal, its eyes stare from a height of over twenty feet, or six
meters. Michelangelo knew that the figure—so large, and so strong, its muscles finely tuned, the
veins defined on its hands— carried a political message as well. It symbolized the city's freedom
from foreign domination and from the rule of tyrants. For 370 years, until 1873, it stood in a spe-
cially designed spot near the entrance of Florence's city hall, defending the city government from
all who would dare threaten it. It was eventually moved to the Accademia Gallery in Florence to
protect it from the greatest tyrant of all: the weather.

David is not only a giant but a sculptural triumph in its own right. It was carved from an
enormous sixteen-foot, or five-meter, block of marble that had been quarried forty years earlier,
before Michelangelo was even born. The block was full of cracks, so many that no one had dared
take a chisel to it. Even Leonardo da Vinci had turned down the problem stone. But Michelangelo
took it on. In all likelihood he understood that if he could successfully make his sculpture from it,
his artistic and cultural power would be as
great as was the historical David's eventual
military and political might. Both became
giants in their time.

David
MICHELANGELO
Marble
Height: 13 feet, 5 inches/4.09 meters
1501–4

1000 B.C.

500 B.C.

0

A.D. 500

A.D. 1000

A.D. 1500

A.D. 2000

1000 B.C.

500 B.C.

0

A.D. 500

A.D. 1000

A.D. 1500

A.D. 2000

Mona Lisa
LEONARDO DA VINCI

Oil on wood
30¼ x 21 inches / 76.8 x 53.3 centimeters
1503–5

No Renaissance painting has fascinated viewers over the centuries more than Leonardo da Vinci's *Mona Lisa.* To many, her smile seems mysterious and knowing, as if she holds some eternal truth. On the other hand, her eyes appear glassy, blurred at the corners, as if, just a moment ago, she had been crying, hurt by some trivial insult or meaningless joke. She seems caught up in both the present moment and everlasting time. She conveys a complex beauty—both the beauty of a real woman and the spiritual beauty of an eternal soul.

Mona Lisa was the wife of Francesco del Gioconda, a prominent businessman in Florence, Italy, and the painting was known for years not as *Mona Lisa* but as *La Gioconda*. When Mona Lisa posed for Leonardo, the artist hired musicians and clowns to keep her entertained as she remained still for the long hours the painting required.

When Leonardo left Florence for France, he took the painting with him. Very few people ever saw it, and he continued to work on it until his death in 1519. Even though we know that the painting fascinated its artist as much as or more than it fascinates us today, maybe we read too much mystery into it. Maybe the *Mona Lisa* is nothing more than a very good portrait and Leonardo was simply in love with his model, or maybe he thought of the painting as somehow a failure. And perhaps this is the definition of a masterpiece: a work of art that is larger than any one person's view of it, larger even than the artist's.

OIL PAINTING

Oil paint can be blended right on the canvas to create a range of light and color. It can be molded and shaped to create bumps. Or it can be thinned with turpentine to become almost transparent. The oil is also very slow to dry, so artists can rework the paintings as many times as they want.

Musée du Louvre, Paris, France.
© Erich Lessing/Art Resource, New York.

The young artist Raphael arrived in Florence in 1504 only to find Michelangelo and Leonardo da Vinci engaged in a contest to see who could paint the greatest battle scene. While the outcome of the two masters' competition was never finally decided—and neither work survives today—Raphael learned much from them both and, in many ways, became an even better painter than either of them.

Raphael stayed in Florence for a little over four years, and during that time he painted seventeen Madonnas, or portraits of Mary with the child Jesus. *The Small Cowper Madonna* is one of these. The realism of the portrayal of the mother and child—the round curves and soft folds of their features—mirror Michelangelo's attention to the details of human anatomy. Mary's right hand is poised on her lap in a position remarkably similar to Leonardo's *Mona Lisa.* Her hands, especially the hand supporting the baby with its outstretched thumb, affirm her gentleness. Her distant gaze suggests that she knows what fate awaits her child.

But where the *Mona Lisa* is dark and mysterious, with stormy mountains and jagged rocks in the background, this painting is full of light and clarity. Mother and child sit in a landscape that is carefully cultivated and civilized. The green grass suggests that it might be spring or early summer, and the two are enjoying the full warmth of the day. Whatever Mary knows of her child's future, now is not the time to ponder its significance. The painting is a celebration of the child's innocence and the mother's love, nothing more nor less.

The Small Cowper Madonna
RAPHAEL
Oil on panel
23 3/8 x 17 3/8 inches/59.5 x 44.1 centimeters
c. 1505

1000 B.C.

500 B.C.

0

A.D. 500

A.D. 1000

A.D. 1500

A.D. 2000

Still Life with Flowers, Goblet, Dried Fruit, and Pretzels

CLARA PEETERS

Oil on panel

19³/₄ x 25¹/₄ inches/50.2 x 64.1 centimeters

1611

Museo del Prado, Madrid, Spain. © Scala/Art Resource, New York.

In the sixteenth and seventeenth centuries in Holland and Belgium, still-life painting became especially important. Tables with plates full of food, pitchers of drink, and vases overflowing with flowers all symbolized to the merchant class who bought these paintings their own wealth and well-being.

Clara Peeters's *Still Life with Flowers, Goblet, Dried Fruit, and Pretzels* is an example of a "breakfast piece," showing a typical northern European breakfast. The pretzels are an interesting addition.

The interlaced form of the pretzel was designed in about A.D. 610 by a monk who formed a strip of dough into the shape of a child's arms folded in prayer. He called it a *pretiola,* Latin for "little reward," and he gave one to children as a prize for learning their prayers. Pretzels also came to hold an honored place as the wedding knot in the marriage ceremony.

The pretzels in Peeters's painting help us understand that this still life is a sort of family portrait. They suggest that this breakfast serves a family where the children are rewarded for learning their prayers and the parents live together in peace and happiness. And Peeters herself looks on with contentment—her tiny self-portrait can be seen in a reflection on the goblet at the center and again (only using a magnifying glass!) in multiple reflections on the pewter pitcher behind the pretzels.

1000 B.C.

5000 B.C.

0

A.D. 500

A.D. 1000

A.D. 1500

A.D. 2000

1000 B.C.

500 B.C.

0

A.D. 500

A.D. 1000

A.D. 1500

*

A.D. 2000

Beginning in 1494 Mughal emperors from Central Asia ruled most of northern India. They brought with them strong Islamic traditions, including the art of illustrating books. The emperor Akbar, who ruled from 1556 to 1605, created a royal workshop where young painters were trained as apprentices.

The first thing the young apprentices learned to do was to make their own paints and brushes. Brushes were made from the hairs of squirrels' tails. The hairs were arranged to taper from a thick base to a single hair at the tip. This allowed the artists to paint with broad strokes, if they laid the brush on its side, and to use the finest of all possible lines, if they painted with the single squirrel-hair tip.

Jahangir in Darbar
ABUL HASAN
AND MANOHAR
Gouache on paper
13 5/8 x 7 5/8 inches/35 x 20 centimeters
c. 1620

Akbar's son, Jahangir, was emperor in the years 1605–27. *Jahangir in Darbar* was painted by his court workshop. A *darbar* is an audience, or a gathering of people who wish to speak with the emperor. The emperor Jahangir sits on a balcony between the columns at the top of the painting. He turns to talk to his son, who will be the next emperor. Below them, in the court-yard, are people from throughout India and beyond. Some have come on elephants and others on horseback. The colors of their skin and the different designs of their clothing show where they're from. Among the group is a visitor from Europe, dressed in a black robe and tight-fitting hat. He is as welcome in the crowd as everyone else, which shows the Mughal emperor's interest in all things foreign.

The emperor Jahangir's workshop provides us with an image of the emperor's openness to all peoples and all ideas. And he is teaching his son the same thing: acknowledge everyone and let the viewpoints of all be heard.

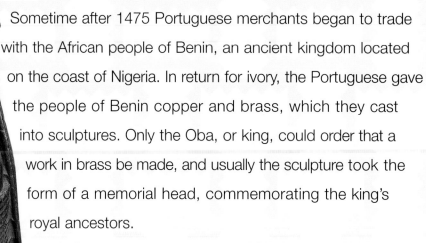

1000 B.C.

500 B.C.

0

A.D. 500

A.D. 1000

A.D. 1500

A.D. 2000

Sometime after 1475 Portuguese merchants began to trade with the African people of Benin, an ancient kingdom located on the coast of Nigeria. In return for ivory, the Portuguese gave the people of Benin copper and brass, which they cast into sculptures. Only the Oba, or king, could order that a work in brass be made, and usually the sculpture took the form of a memorial head, commemorating the king's royal ancestors.

All the brass heads depict the ancestor in royal costume. A coral-bead crown and a high, cylindrical beaded necklace that conceals the chin symbolize the king's authority. But it is the head itself that is most important. For the people of Benin, the head is the place that allows us to organize our behavior so that we thrive in our lives. The head, so the saying goes, "leads one through life." The welfare of the family thus depends upon the head of the father. The welfare of the people depends upon the head of the Oba. In the head lies the Oba's identity and spirit, and so also, the identity and spirit of the people.

So similar are the many Oba heads that have survived, it seems likely that they are not actual portraits. Instead, they probably represent an ideal "type"—the "king," the great ancestor whose image carries the power of the past into the present.

Head of an Oba

Brass and iron
Height: 13 1/8 inches / 33.3 centimeters
c. 1700–1800

Mandan Battle Scene Hide Painting

Tanned buffalo hide, dyed porcupine quills, and pigment
7 feet, 10 inches x 8 feet, 6 inches
2.44 x 2.65 meters
c. 1797–1805

The Mandan, or "people of the first man," lived in the Great Plains along the Heart River, a tributary of the Missouri River near present-day Bismark, North Dakota. Like the other Native American tribes of the region, they hunted buffalo and used the hides for clothing. But they did not follow the buffalo herds wherever they roamed. Instead, they lived in permanent villages. Their lodges were dome-shaped and earth-covered. Outside the walls of the villages, they planted corn, beans, pumpkins, and sunflowers.

This buffalo-hide robe was painted to honor a Mandan victory in a battle fought against the Sioux in 1797. It would have been worn over the shoulders of the chief whose victory it celebrates. He is shown with a pipe wearing an eagle-feather headdress. The battle itself is shown in twenty-two different episodes. The warriors are armed with bows and arrows, clubs, lances, and rifles. Down the center of the robe is a strip of colored porcupine quills.

The robe was collected by Meriwether Lewis and William Clark on their 1803–6 expedition up the Missouri River and across Montana, Idaho, and the Oregon territory to the Pacific Ocean. It was sent to President Thomas Jefferson as a present, and Jefferson hung the robe in the entrance hall to his home in Virginia.

The Mandan, however, did not survive as well as the robe. After the visit of Lewis and Clark, smallpox devastated them. In 1837, after a second outbreak of smallpox, only 125 Mandans survived. Today, there are only a few full-blooded Mandan left, and their culture is practically extinct.

1000 B.C.

500 B.C.

0

A.D. 500

A.D. 1000

A.D. 1500

*

A.D. 2000

Hokusai's GREAT WAVE is part of a Japanese printmaking tradition known as UKIYO-E, "pictures of the floating world."
It celebrates the momentary beauty of the world and the joy of life.

Between 1823 and 1829 the Japanese artist Katsushika Hokusai created a series of prints entitled Thirty-Six Views of Mount Fuji. It is the most successful series of prints ever made. The woodblocks were printed over and over again until they were worn out, and then they were recarved and printed again. In all of the prints, Mount Fuji is seen in the far distance, rising 12,388 feet, or 3,776 meters, above the Pacific coastline just to the southwest of Tokyo.

In *The Great Wave off Kanagawa,* one of the prints from the series, a giant wave rises to an enormous height, ready to crash down on two boats. The wave seems ready to swallow even the distant Mount Fuji. The nearest boat crashes through a smaller wave that looks like a miniature Fuji.

This is a good example of perspective. The wave looks huge because it's close and the faraway mountain looks small. But really, the mountain looms over everything. In real life, the mountain is huge, and the wave is small. But in the moment shown in the painting, the mountain hardly seems to matter. Life comes down to this moment, and it is dangerous beyond belief. For the people in the boats, nothing can be seen but the waves, nothing heard but the roar of the ocean. The question is how to get from this moment to the next.

Mount Fuji, on the other hand, is still, quiet, never-changing. One meaning of "Fuji" is "eternal life," and for centuries the Japanese have considered the mountain a symbol of immortality. Nature endures, Hokusai's print suggests, and people must endure whatever nature sends their way, or else perish.

WOODBLOCK PRINTMAKING

To make a woodblock print a drawing is made on tissue-thin paper and pressed onto a block of wood. The wood is cut away so only the lines of the picture are raised. Finally, the block is brushed with ink, a piece of paper is pressed on top, and rubbed to transfer the ink from the wood to the paper.

The Great Wave
off Kanagawa
KATSUSHIKA HOKUSAI
Woodblock print
10 x 15 inches/25 x 37.1 centimeters
c. 1823–29

1000 B.C.

500 B.C.

0

A.D. 500

A.D. 1000

A.D. 1500

*

A.D. 2000

1000 B.C.

500 B.C.

0

A.D. 500

A.D. 1000

A.D. 1500

*

A.D. 2000

By the middle of the eighteenth century, French trappers and fur traders had become a regular feature of the Missouri and Mississippi Valleys. But as American settlements moved westward and the steamboat became popular, the traders were forced farther and farther west. George Caleb Bingham's 1845 painting *Fur Traders Descending the Missouri* marks the end of an era. The time is early evening, and the sun is setting not only on these two lone figures but on the fur trade itself.

Fur Traders Descending the Missouri
GEORGE CALEB BINGHAM
Oil on canvas
29¼ x 36¼ inches/55.2 x 92.7 centimeters
1845

Bingham was not only a painter but also a politician who served as a Missouri state representative in the late 1840s.

Contentedly smoking his pipe, a French trapper guides his canoe down the river. We can tell he is French by his striped shirt with its billowing sleeves, but Bingham's original title for the painting—*French Trader and His Half-Breed Son*—confirms this, and it also gives the identity of the boy leaning over the pile of furs in the middle of the boat. Many French trappers married Native American women and had children with them. The boy wears a French shirt and pants like his father, and his hair is cut short, but beneath his elbow is a Native American beadwork shoulder bag. In front of him is a duck that he has most likely just shot with the gun in his arms—perhaps it will be their dinner. At the front of the boat, on a leash, is a furry animal that many believe to be a bear cub—which is the Missouri state symbol. In fact, the state's name is a Native American word meaning "people who use canoes." But a new Missouri, of steamboats and riverboats, businessmen and bankers, was about to dawn. These two traders look out of the painting at us as if we are passing them by, headed upstream into the future as they row downstream into the past.

At first glance, the title of Edouard Manet's painting *The Railroad* seems odd. A young woman sits against an iron fence. She looks out of the painting, a dog in her lap and a book in her hand. Next to her a young girl stands with her back to us, peering through the fence. What is she looking at? Steam and smoke fill the air. In fact, she is looking down at a train pulling out of the St. Lazare Station in Paris.

Manet knew these two young women. The older one is Victorine Meurent, Manet's favorite model. The younger is Suzanne Hirsch, the daughter of one of Manet's friends. The painting is set in Suzanne's garden overlooking the station.

The two are like positive and negative images of one another. Victorine is dressed in blue, with white trim; Suzanne in white, with blue trim. Victorine wears a hat, with her hair down; Suzanne is hatless, with her hair up. Victorine's neckline is cut at a severe angle; Suzanne's is a soft curve. Victorine wears a ribbon around her neck; Suzanne uses one to hold up her hair. And, of course, Victorine faces us, while Suzanne turns away. They represent the contrast between youth and maturity. Victorine is the woman Suzanne will grow up to be.

Suzanne stares through the fence at the departing train as if dreaming of adventure. Victorine has also been dreaming of escape, lost in the world of her book. But neither can escape their world. This is the meaning of the iron fence, which rises like prison bars. The painting shows the limits French society imposed on women in Manet's time.

The Railroad
EDOUARD MANET
Oil on canvas
36 ½ x 45 inches / 93.3 x 111.5 centimeters
1872–73

IMPRESSIONIST PAINTING

"To set down the fleeting impression" was the object of a group of French painters who exhibited together in Paris between 1874 and 1886. They called themselves Impressionists. They painted with thick strokes, often dipping the brush into two or three colors at once and blending them together to capture the momentary effects of light.

1000 B.C.

500 B.C.

0

A.D. 500

A.D. 1000

A.D. 1500

A.D. 2000

1000 B.C.

500 B.C.

0

A.D. 500

A.D. 1000

A.D. 1500

A.D. 2000

Ballet is one of the most difficult dances. It requires extreme physical fitness, as well as unmatched agility and balance. Its various positions, especially *en pointe*—standing on the tiptoes of the ballet slipper—can cause severe physical pain and sometimes lead to permanent disability.

In the 1870s almost all ballet dancers were from the lower classes. Most couldn't read or write.

In Degas's *Dance Class,* dancers rehearse under the watchful gaze of Jules Perrot, who at one time was the greatest male dancer in all of France. Perrot considers a young dancer's position, the beauty of which Degas accentuates by having her leg and arm extend the curve created by the bottom of the foreground dancer's tutu. This young woman, in the very front of the painting, is having her tutu adjusted by her friend behind her. Apparently a flower has fallen out of her hair, and the dancer helping her has stepped on it. The sense of competition is keen, as if anyone might step on anyone else in order to gain the good graces of the master. Young dancers wait in the bleachers with their mothers. A young, dark-haired dancer stands on a chair, her fingers at her lips, looking on with concern.

For Degas, who depicted many ballet scenes, the ballet dancer is a mystery, at once a thing of total beauty, like the flowers she wears in her hair, and also a sweaty, exhausted laborer of modern industry, condemned to endless, repetitive, mind-numbing work.

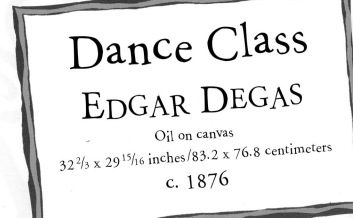

Dance Class
EDGAR DEGAS
Oil on canvas
32 2/3 x 29 15/16 inches / 83.2 x 76.8 centimeters
c. 1876

1000 B.C.

500 B.C.

0

A.D. 500

A.D. 1000

A.D. 1500

A.D. 2000

The painter Mary Cassatt was a very independent woman. Before she was thirty years old, she had trained as a painter at the Pennsylvania Academy of Fine Arts in Philadelphia and had traveled throughout Europe, finally settling in Paris in 1874. There she met and exhibited with the Impressionist painters, including Edgar Degas, Edouard Manet, Claude Monet, and Auguste Renoir. She became especially good friends with Degas.

Cassatt loved to paint mothers and children. And she liked to capture more than just their physical appearance. She wanted to reveal something about their feelings and emotions. *Little Girl in a Blue Armchair* is a perfect example. The little girl is the daughter of friends of Degas. She has thrown herself on the chair, her fashionable tartan skirt pulled up around her waist revealing her petticoats. Her hair is done up.

Little Girl in a Blue Armchair
MARY CASSATT
Oil on canvas
33 x 51 inches/89.5 x 129.8 centimeters
1878

She even seems to have a little rouge on her lips. On the chair next to her is Cassatt's dog.

We can guess her parents have brought her to Cassatt's for the artist to paint her portrait. But she is not interested in posing. She seems hot, bored, even a little defiant. "I don't have to put up with this!" she seems to say. "You can't make me hold still!" And Cassatt apparently agrees. To paint the little girl sitting up properly in a chair, all smiles, would misrepresent her. Cassatt wants to show her spirit and energy. She wants to capture her independence, an independence with which the painter no doubt identifies.

The Umbrellas

AUGUSTE RENOIR

Oil on canvas

71 x 45¼ inches/180 x 115 centimeters

c. 1881–85

We are sometimes asked to become spectators in a painting, characters caught up in the event itself. In Renoir's *The Umbrellas,* the young woman at the left catches our eye. Her dress is plain and simple, much more so than the well-dressed ladies around her. Unlike everyone else in the painting, she is hatless. The basket under her arm is covered with oil cloth, a waterproof fabric that she has drawn across the top to protect whatever is inside—maybe bread for her dinner. But she has no umbrella herself, no protection from the elements. The woman behind her raises her umbrella. It is beginning to rain.

By 1900, Renoir was so crippled by rheumatism that he often could paint only by strapping a brush to his arm.

As viewers, we feel some sympathy for this pretty, young woman. And the little girl with the hoop knows it. We realize that she is watching us as we watch the young woman. Her mother turns to her as if to say, "Come along, dear. It's beginning to rain!" But she wants to see how things turn out. Will we offer the young woman a place under our own umbrella?

Gazing into the world of Renoir's *The Umbrellas,* we are forever caught up in this moment. We will never know what happens next, but the painting leaves us with a sense—or *impression*—of French society in the 1870s and 1880s.

National Gallery, London, England. © National Gallery Collection.
By kind permission of the Board of Trustees, National Gallery, London.

1000 B.C.

500 B.C.

0

A.D. 500

A.D. 1000

A.D. 1500

A.D. 2000

Irises
VINCENT VAN GOGH
Oil on canvas
28 x 36 ³/₄ inches/71.1 x 93.3 centimeters
c. 1889

The art of Vincent van Gogh has always been linked with his emotions. Between the spring of 1888 and his death in July of 1890, he was particularly active, drawing and painting hundreds of works. Some of them were self-portraits, but all of them—landscapes, portraits of friends, and still lifes—revealed his personality. His brush strokes, thick with paint and full of color, seem to say, "Here I am, at work!"

Irises was probably painted in May 1889, about a week after van Gogh decided to seek help for his mental illness and entered a hospital in France. It is a painting of the hospital's garden, a group of blue-and-violet irises in front of a patch of marigolds. A lone white iris rises at the left.

The lonely white iris stands for van Gogh himself, alone in the hospital, far from friends and family, somehow "different" from everybody else. And yet see how all the other irises seem to lean toward the white one, as if recognizing its uniqueness, its genius.

Van Gogh often made a painting a day.

Van Gogh sold only one painting in his lifetime, but he was deeply convinced of his great talent. After his death, his brother's wife began to organize exhibitions of Vincent's work, and eventually many of the paintings were sold, including *Irises,* which was purchased in 1892 for 300 French francs (about U.S.$80). In the hundred years since then, so great has van Gogh's reputation become that in 1988 *Irises* sold at auction for U.S.$53 million.

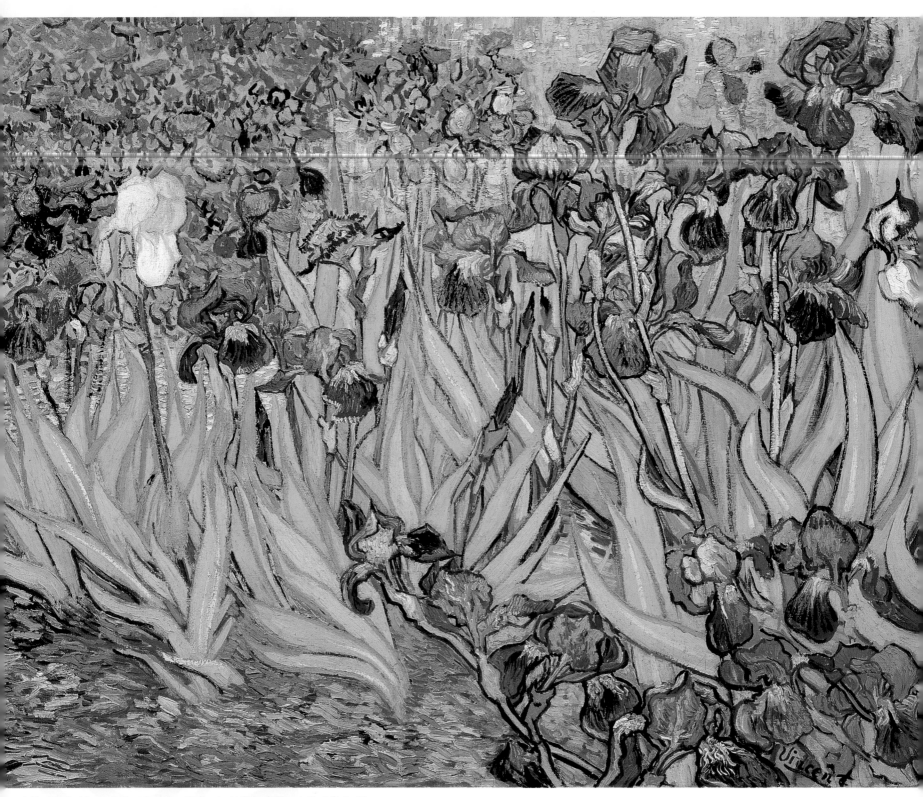

Gauguin 04

MAHANA no Atua

Paul Gauguin, like his friend Vincent van Gogh, painted his emotions. But he expressed these emotions differently than van Gogh. In the art of undeveloped, "primitive" societies, Gauguin discovered a directness and intensity of feeling that he tried to capture in his own work. Convinced that European society was corrupt, he left France for the Polynesian islands, particularly Tahiti and the Marquesas. When he returned to France, as he sometimes did, he preferred to live in Brittany because, he said, it was more "backward" than the rest of France.

Mahana no atua is Polynesian for "Day of the God." It was painted in France during a twenty-two-month visit in 1893–94 after Gauguin had spent two years in Tahiti. It is a sort of dream-image of the perfection of life in the South Seas.

At the top left of the painting two women in white balance large platters of food on their heads as they walk toward a large sculpture of a god. On the other side, two women in red dance to the music of a pipe played by a figure sitting on the rock before the god. Almost directly behind the god, a couple embraces. The man appears to be European; perhaps it is Gauguin himself.

In the middle of the painting, three figures are arranged beside a pool. Perhaps they are symbols of birth, life, and death. The pool that stretches across the bottom of the painting is ablaze with color—reds and greens, yellows and violets, oranges and blues—the entire spectrum of light, which Gauguin believed to be the life force of the universe.

Mahana no atua
PAUL GAUGUIN
Oil on canvas
26 7/8 x 36 1/8 inches/68.3 x 91.5 centimeters
1894

1000 B.C.

500 B.C.

0

A.D. 500

A.D. 1000

A.D. 1500

A.D. 2000

1000 B.C.

500 B.C.

0

A.D. 500

A.D. 1000

A.D. 1500

*

A.D. 2000

Water Lily Pond

CLAUDE MONET

Oil on canvas

$35\,^{1}/_{8}$ x $38\,^{3}/_{8}$ inches/89.2 x 92.4 centimeters

1904

Of all the Impressionist painters, Claude Monet was the most dedicated to capturing light. In the 1890s he would pack up his paints every day, walk into the countryside around the little town of Giverny, north of Paris, where he lived, and paint grainstacks in every season of the year, at every time of day. The resulting series of paintings, called Grainstacks, recorded *le temps,* which in French means three different things—the "weather," the "time of day," and "the times" or "era" in which we live.

Even as he was painting the grainstacks, he was thinking about building a garden on some land he had purchased across from his house beside a river. He thought he might convert a pond there into a Japanese-style garden with an arched bridge at one end. He ordered water lilies from a garden-supply catalogue, thinking they might be a good addition. Little did he realize that the lilies would become the main subject of his paintings for the next thirty years of his life.

Before he could plant this water lily pond, Monet had to appease the local farmers, who were afraid his exotic plants might poison the cattle that drank downstream.

Monet would call his water lily paintings "landscapes of water." Water, especially the still water of a pond, is a very difficult thing to paint. It is both transparent—you can see through it—and reflective. It mirrors, upside down, the world around it. The water lilies are important to the paintings not only because they are beautiful but because, floating on top of the water, they help us see just where the surface of the water is.

For Monet, the water lilies are islands of peace. They offer a much-needed resting place from the rush and noise of our modern times.

Denver Art Museum, Denver, Colorado, U.S.A. Funds from Helen Dill bequest, 1935.14. Photograph © 2003 Denver Art Museum.

1000 B.C.

500 B.C.

0

A.D. 500

A.D. 1000

A.D. 1500

A.D. 2000

Improvisation 30 (Cannons)

WASSILY KANDINSKY

Oil on canvas

43 ¼ x 43 ¼ inches / 109.8 x 111 centimeters

1913

Wassily Kandinsky is considered by many to be the first painter to paint in a completely abstract manner—that is, to create paintings without any reference to reality. He called these paintings *Improvisations.* They were, he said, "largely unconscious," revealing his "inner character" or "spirit."

But *Improvisation 30* is not completely abstract. It was painted just before World War I, when all of Europe was afraid of what was about to come. Cannons explode from the bottom right of the painting. They seem to be aiming at a domed structure. Other buildings can be seen behind the cannon. Two mountains loom over the scene. Or perhaps this is a view of Kandinsky's native Moscow. The domed building on the left looks like the churches of the Kremlin. Kandinsky, we know, strongly believed that the Russian capital would be the new center of Christianity after the destruction of the world that many Russian faithful thought would occur soon after 1900. In that case, this is a picture of the Russian triumph to come, not the artist's fear of the coming war.

Either way, the painting is full of emotion. Kandinsky once compared his paintings to looking at a chandelier at a concert hall and then closing your eyes. Colors dance in the darkness behind your eyelids as the music plays. "Color is the keyboard," he wrote, "the eyes are the hammers, the soul is the piano with many strings. The artist is the hand that plays, touching one key or another…to cause vibrations in the soul."

The Art Institute of Chicago, Chicago, Illinois, U.S.A. Arthur Jerome Eddy Memorial Collection. 1931.511. Image © The Art Institute of Chicago/Artists Rights Society (ARS), New York

Many people consider Pablo Picasso the greatest artist of the twentieth century. He was certainly one of the most inventive. From the time he first moved to Paris in 1900, at the age of nineteen, until his death in 1973, he explored almost every imaginable style, from the most realistic to the most abstract. He worked in almost every medium—he made paintings and drawings and sculptures in stone, bronze, and wood, and explored almost every technique of printmaking. He invented *collage*—the technique of pasting paper and other materials onto a work of art. And he was the founder of a new style of painting called Cubism, in which the painting's subject matter was "flattened" into geometric forms.

Man with a Pipe
PABLO PICASSO
Oil on canvas
51 ¼ x 35 ¼ inches / 130.2 x 89.5 centimeters
1915

Man with a Pipe is a fully Cubist painting. The man sits in an armchair holding his pipe, but it is as if the entire scene, including the room itself, has been flattened out on the canvas. Consider the man's face: his moustache and mouth are plainly visible, and so is his right eye. But his ears are flattened far to the side. His left eye is the round white circle with a dot in it just above his left ear. His eyebrow is more feather than eyebrow.

Picasso is having fun. At the lower right the man holds his pipe in his hand. His other hand rests, at the lower left, on the arm of the chair. Behind it is a piece of floor tile. We look up, we look down. What is in back comes forward. What is in front disappears. All makes for the flat design of Picasso's Cubist portrait.

Mexican muralist Diego Rivera believed that his art should reflect the political and social realities of his country. He received a scholarship to study art in Europe in 1907, and he stayed there for fourteen years, studying the abstract modernism of Picasso. But after the Mexican Revolution in 1910, he became more and more convinced that he didn't want his paintings to be abstract; he wanted them to be easily understandable to the Mexican peasants and workers who had fought and won in the revolution. In the decade after he returned home in 1921, he painted 124 murals showing the struggle between rich and poor people in Mexico.

Sugar Cane is one of eight portable murals that Rivera painted for a 1931 exhibition at the Museum of Modern Art in New York. It shows Mexican peasants chopping and bundling sugar cane. In the front of the painting, other workers, including a child, cut coconuts from the trees and carry them off in baskets. A foreman employed by the landowner, with a gun at his hip, sits on his horse, pointing a whipping stick at the laborers. In the background, lying in the hammock and with dogs sleeping beneath his feet, is the landowner. He also has a whip in his hand. This is an image of the oppression of the poor by the rich, of the near-slavery conditions they were subjected to.

But Rivera's realistic portrayal of the lives of his people is also a celebration of their ability to endure through all ages. The simplicity of the features of the man carrying the coconuts suggests that he is a direct descendant of the Olmec rulers whose giant heads once adorned the pyramids at La Venta.

Sugar Cane
JOSÉ DIEGO
MARIA RIVERA
Fresco
$57^{1}/_{8}$ x $84^{1}/_{8}$ inches/145.1 x 213.7 centimeters
1931

1000 B.C.

500 B.C.

0

A.D. 500

A.D. 1000

A.D. 1500

A.D. 2000

1000 B.C.

500 B.C.

0

A.D. 500

A.D. 1000

A.D. 1500

*

A.D. 2000

In 1941, at the age of twenty-four, Jacob Lawrence, a young African-American painter who was living in a run-down New York City building, with no heat or running water, painted a series of sixty paintings. They tell the story of the flight of millions of African Americans from the rural South to the urban North during and after World War I. African Americans were the largest source of labor during the war, and many Northern industrialists gave them free passage north in return for their work. It was an attractive option for the migrants who were generally very poor. Their crops had been ravaged by the boll weevil. And, because of the war, food had doubled in price. Discrimination in the South left many feeling they were no longer safe. So many African Americans migrated north that whole communities were essentially abandoned.

Even though Lawrence's paintings are all individually very small, taken together and viewed around a single room, they tell an amazing story of a migration of people that changed American history. Each painting has a caption that describes the scene Lawrence has chosen to paint. In the panel shown here, masses of people, headed north to Chicago, New York, Pittsburgh, and St. Louis, wait patiently in a Southern train station (there were no airports in those days). In other paintings, Lawrence shows the harsh living conditions that the African Americans discovered in the North, the run-down tenement houses and cramped quarters that led to a high rate of disease, particularly tuberculosis. Lawrence also paints the race riots that resulted from the conflict between the African Americans and white workers, who were threatened by this influx of this new, less expensive labor force. But, the series concludes, African Americans had better educational facilities in the North, and, perhaps above all, the freedom to vote. As a result, "the migrants kept coming," and benches in train stations across the South continued to be full, just like the one illustrated here.

The Migration of the Negro, No. 32
The railroad stations were crowded with people leaving for the North
JACOB LAWRENCE
Casein tempera on hardboard
12 x 18 inches/30.5 x 45.7 centimeters
1941

Jacob Lawrence was the first African-American artist
to be represented by a major gallery in the United States.
His work is now in nearly two hundred museum collections.

Nighthawks

EDWARD HOPPER

Oil on canvas

30 x 60 inches/84.1 x 152.4 centimeters

1942

In Edward Hopper's *Nighthawks,* three people sit alone in an all-night diner, drinking coffee and smoking cigarettes. The woman looks at her nails. The man next to her seems to be talking with the waiter. A third man, his back to us, is hunched over his coffee, alone with his thoughts. The name of the place, as we can read at the top of the diner, is Phillies.

Hopper's painting captures a moment of American life that seems as bleak and empty as the streets outside the diner. Hopper and his wife, Jo, usually named every character in his paintings and made up stories about how they came to be in the scenes. The result is that the paintings look like movie stills—"frozen moments" in an imaginary film. Hopper wants the wide format of the painting to remind us of a movie screen, as if we are viewing a scene from some 1940s murder mystery. Perhaps the man is a detective, asking the waiter if he has seen someone or heard something. Or maybe these are gangsters in some crime drama.

When Hopper had his first solo exhibition in 1920, not a single painting sold, but just four years later, his work was so popular his exhibitions would sell out.

Even though it looks drab, *Nighthawks* is a beautifully arranged painting. The diner is rectangular, the three people at the counter are framed in a rectangular window, and the painting itself is a rectangle. Hopper's greatest talent was his ability to make even the most common scene seem almost magical.

1000 B.C.

500 B.C.

0

A.D. 500

A.D. 1000

A.D. 1500

A.D. 2000

1000 B.C.	
500 B.C.	
0	
A.D. 500	
A.D. 1000	
A.D. 1500	
A.D. 2000	

Convergence

JACKSON POLLOCK

Oil on canvas
7 feet, 9½ inches x 12 feet, 11 inches
2.4 x 3.9 meters
1952

In the 1930s, in both Europe and the United States, one of the most important movements in art was called Surrealism. The Surrealists believed in a reality beyond the reality of everyday life—a sur-reality. They were interested in dreams because, they believed, dreams showed what was hidden inside people's minds. In order to get to the hidden parts of themselves, Surrealist painters tried to draw or paint without planning first or even thinking while they were working. They would just try to let the art come out of them automatically.

American painter Jackson Pollock was fascinated by Surrealism. He wanted to find a way to paint so that his own inner emotions could find their way onto the canvas with-

out his own thoughts getting in the way. He took sticks, trowels, knives—anything that was at hand—dipped them in thick, dripping paint, and flung the paint onto the canvas. He tried to turn off his thoughts and move like a dancer around his canvas, which was laid out on the floor. "When I am in my painting," he said, "I am not aware of what I'm doing." In painting *Convergence,* he started out with a thick, heaped up swirl of black paint and then dripped trickles of white, yellow, red, and blue over it.

For Pollock, painting was not the thing he made, but the process of *making.* For him, "art" was the process of expressing himself in the act of painting. For this reason, he has often been called an "action painter" or Abstract Expressionist.

Georgia O'Keeffe is one of the most popular and important painters of the twentieth century. She's especially famous for her magnificent flower paintings. She's also remarkable for possessing such a free spirit in an age when it was not as acceptable as it is today for a woman to be independent.

O'Keeffe loved New Mexico, and from 1929 until her death in 1986, she spent at least every summer there, moving permanently to an adobe house in Abiquiu in 1949. *Ladder to the Moon* was painted in 1958 at the Abiquiu house. "At the Ranch house," O'Keeffe said, "there is a strong handmade ladder to the roof, and when I first lived there I climbed it several times a day to look at the world all 'round—the miles of cliff behind, the wide line of low mountains with a higher narrow flat top.... One evening I was waiting for a friend and stood leaning against the ladder. The sky was a pale greenish blue, the high moon looking white in the evening sky. Painting the ladder had been in my mind for a long time, and there it was." The ladder floats in the sky as if reaching for the moon.

Ladders are an important symbol in the Navajo communities of New Mexico, which O'Keeffe knew well. They lean up against the sides of the Navajo *pueblos* so people can climb to the roofs. For the Navajo, they bind together Mother Earth and the heavenly skies above and represent the unity of all things. Likewise, O'Keeffe's ladder floats between earth and sky, between our reality and our dreams.

Ladder to the Moon
GEORGIA O'KEEFFE
Oil on canvas
40 x 30 inches/101.6 x 76.2 centimeters
1958

1000 B.C.

500 B.C.

0

A.D. 500

A.D. 1000

A.D. 1500

A.D. 2000

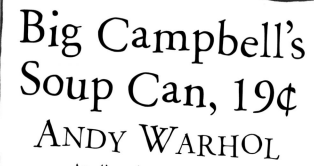

Big Campbell's Soup Can, 19¢
ANDY WARHOL
Acrylic and pencil on canvas
72 x 54 ½ inches/182.9 x 138.4 centimeters
1962

For Andy Warhol, a painting of a Campbell's soup can was a kind of all-American still life. In the early 1960s, when he made one Campbell's Soup Can painting after another—Beef Noodle, Chicken with Rice, Vegetable Beef, Bean with Bacon, Tomato—four out of every five cans of soup sold in America were Campbell's. Like many American kids born during and after World War II, Warhol had grown up on Campbell's soup. Whole aisles of grocery stores were lined with the can's red-and-white label, and when Warhol painted a giant canvas filled with an enormous stack of one hundred cans, it was a scene familiar to most Americans.

But even though people liked to eat Campbell's soup, they didn't think a painting of a soup can was art. When Warhol first exhibited his soup can paintings in 1962, at a Los Angeles gallery, other artists and the public were angry. The gallery next door filled its front window with stacks of real Campbell's soup cans and advertised "the real thing" for 29¢ a can.

Before Warhol became a famous artist, he worked as an illustrator for fashion magazines like MADEMOISELLE, GLAMOUR, VOGUE, and HARPER'S BAZAAR.

What upset most people was Warhol's way of painting. The pieces looked more like billboard advertisements than paintings. He even simplified the gold Campbell's medallion to a plain yellow circle. There seemed to be nothing "personal" about them, no sense of self-expression or feeling. Where, people asked, was the "art" in that?

Warhol turned the question around. Why isn't a soup can art? By bringing soup cans, Brillo boxes, Coca-Cola bottles, dollar bills, and popular images of movie stars into "the world of art," doesn't Warhol transform them into art? And don't they reflect our age, as art has always reflected its times?

The Son of Man

RENÉ MAGRITTE

Oil on canvas

45 5/8 x 35 inches / 116 x 89 centimeters

1964

By all accounts, René Magritte lived a humdrum, even uneventful life in Brussels, Belgium. Each day he walked his dog, Loulou, to the grocery store. Each afternoon he visited a local café where he spent hours with the chess players. He never had a studio; he painted in a small room next to his bedroom. He habitually dressed in a black coat, a black bowler hat, a white shirt, and a tie.

But he did not paint in any humdrum, uneventful way. His paintings are mysterious images that defy ordinary logic and common sense. In *The Son of Man,* an apple hangs in mid-air, blocking our view of the man's face behind it. The man could be Magritte. He is dressed the way Magritte always dressed. But he could also be anyone—and everyone. He is universal.

We can't see the man's face, and he can't see us. All the man can see is the apple. It makes up his entire "world view." Or does it? Where, in the space between us, does this apple, defying all the laws of gravity, float? Perhaps it is directly in front of *our* face, not his. And what does it mean? Is it symbolic of an apple from the garden of Eden? Or is it just an ordinary apple, floating in space?

Magritte's paintings never answer questions. They just ask them. We are, of course, all the sons and daughters of "man." But so is the painting, as its title states. It is what Magritte has made. His paintings are his children. They inherit his traits. He lives on through their presence.

This painting is, finally, about his way of seeing. What is it, he asks, that we see in a work of art? Our reflection? Our history? Or is art, like this apple, an illusion, hanging in the air between us and our world? Maybe that's what makes art so delectable for Magritte. It's both real and an illusion. It's a dreamscape. Perhaps, most of all, it makes our dreams real.

GLOSSARY

Abstract art Art that uses colors, shapes, and patterns to express a feeling or an idea, sometimes in recognizable pictures and sometimes not.

Allegory In a work of art, a human figure or an object that stands for an idea or concept.

Amphora A type of vase used to carry wine.

Apprentice A person working under a skilled craftsman to learn the trade.

Bronze A hard metal made of tin, copper, and iron.

Calligraphy The art of handwriting.

Casting The process of creating sculpture by pouring hot liquid metal into a mold. Once the metal hardens the mold is taken off.

Ceramic An object made from clay and fired in a kiln or baked.

Colossal Massive in size.

Cubism A style of painting in which the subject matter is represented in flat, geometric forms.

Fresco The technique of wall-painting in which paint is applied to areas of wet plaster.

Gesso A base coat that is spread on a surface before painting.

Gilded Overlaid with a thin layer of gold.

Gold leaf A thin layer of gold.

Hieroglyphs Symbols used in the writing system of ancient Egypt.

Mummy A body preserved for burial in the manner of the ancient Egyptians.

Mural A painting applied directly to a wall.

Ocher A yellow-brown or reddish-brown clay or pigment.

Oculus A round opening or "eye" at the top of a dome.

Oil paint A kind of paint in which pigment is mixed with oil.

Palette A thin board on which an artist lays out and mixes paint.

Perspective The art of painting or drawing to give the illusion of distance or depth.

Pigment A substance that provides color to paint, usually a dry powder taken from plants or minerals.

Prehistoric Taking place during a period before recorded history.

Renaissance The period of European history between the 1300s and the 1600s, known for its abundance of art and learning.

Replica A precise copy of a work of art.

Sarcophagus A coffin.

Scroll A roll of paper or parchment with writing or a decorative design.

Sculpture A three-dimensional work of art.

Shrine An honored place often containing religious artifacts.

Slip A mixture of clay and water used in ceramics.

Tapestry A cloth woven with a decorative design.

Tempera A kind of paint in which pigment is mixed with some kind of gum or glue, usually egg yolk, to make it dry hard.

Tomb A vault or grave for burial.

Vessel A container such as a cup or pot.

Watercolor A kind of paint in which pigment is thinned with water.

INDEX